SO-BOB-748

in

Story by
Brad Bluth

Illustrations by
Toby Bluth

Ideals Publishing Corporation
Milwaukee, Wisconsin

Copyright © MCMLXXXIV by Bluth Brothers Productions
All rights reserved. Printed and bound in U.S.A.
Published simultaneously in Canada.

ISBN 0-8249-8062-X

This sunny spring day
in the best of weather
two friends sit discussing
a chess game together.

On the left is Jack Rabbit
who's set up the game
with kings, knights and castles
on a checkerboard frame.

Bo Bo the monkey
is learning to play.
Though he's trying his best,
this could take all day.

Jack's explaining the game.
Bo Bo's not comprehending,
but not to look dumb
the monkey's pretending.

Then suddenly they stop —
a noise turns them 'round.
Whistle, wiz, whine,
calls a well-known sound.

Is this a cyclone,
this dazzling dust cloud
coming their way
and getting real loud?

No, this is Dicky,
just down the lane.
Dicky Duck, Mr. Luck,
as fast as a train.

Atop a sleek skateboard
fixed with jet thrusters
leaving wistful white trails
of smoke-cloud clusters.

He glides to a stop, dismounts with a hop,
never missing a beat.
Dicky says, "Hi!" as he straightens his tie
and kicks the road dust from his feet.

Bo Bo says "Wanna play? It's a mighty fine day!"
"We've a chess game here," adds Jack.
"I can't. I told mother I'd watch new baby brother.
I'm in charge and must hurry right back."

"New baby brother!"
Jack and Bo Bo reply.
"Let's forget this game
and go see the new guy."

The Buddies go to Dicky's
for their babysitting chore.
Dicky says his brother's inside
as they all go through the door.

And there lies an egg;
Dicky's brother is "inside."
But Bo Bo's seen a baby,
and he's seen an egg fried.

"This egg's not for eating,"
Jack says, "It's alive!
If we wait and we watch,
pretty soon he'll arrive."

"Well, let's let him out!"
Bo Bo bangs on the egg.
Jack grabs Bo Bo's tail.
Dicky grabs Bo Bo's leg.

Dicky calms Bo Bo down.
Jack explains things really plain,
so slowly the idea
will sink into Bo Bo's brain.

"We'll be just like knights
with a noble trust.
To protect this baby
we will do what we must.

Bo Bo squares his shoulders,
and he stands erect.
The idea is clear;
he's here to protect!

Now, not far away
lay a railroad liner,
owned by Rim Rat the Weeze,
named the Atomic Egg Diner.

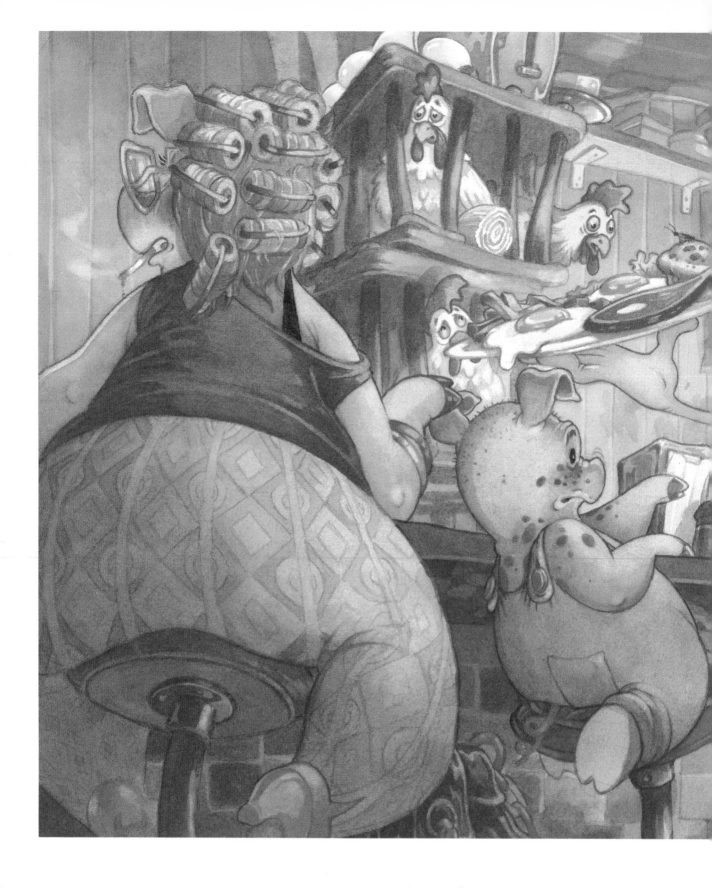

For free eggs, Rat keeps hens
caged up in his kitchen.
And they're forced to lay eggs
till the poor hens are twitchin'.

Well, this Rat fixes eggs
of every description,
and most of his eggs
are eggs he's been snitchin'!

Some eggs are rare
like those of the duck.
And the Weeze knows duck eggs
bring a very big buck.

So he's hired an egg scout,
a fly called Buzz.
And scouting eggs
is just what Buzz does.

Buzz bursts in
through the back diner door,
buzzing "Boss! Boss!
I just found one more!

"This egg's babysat
by three kids *where it's at,*
But I have a plan
that can sure fix that.

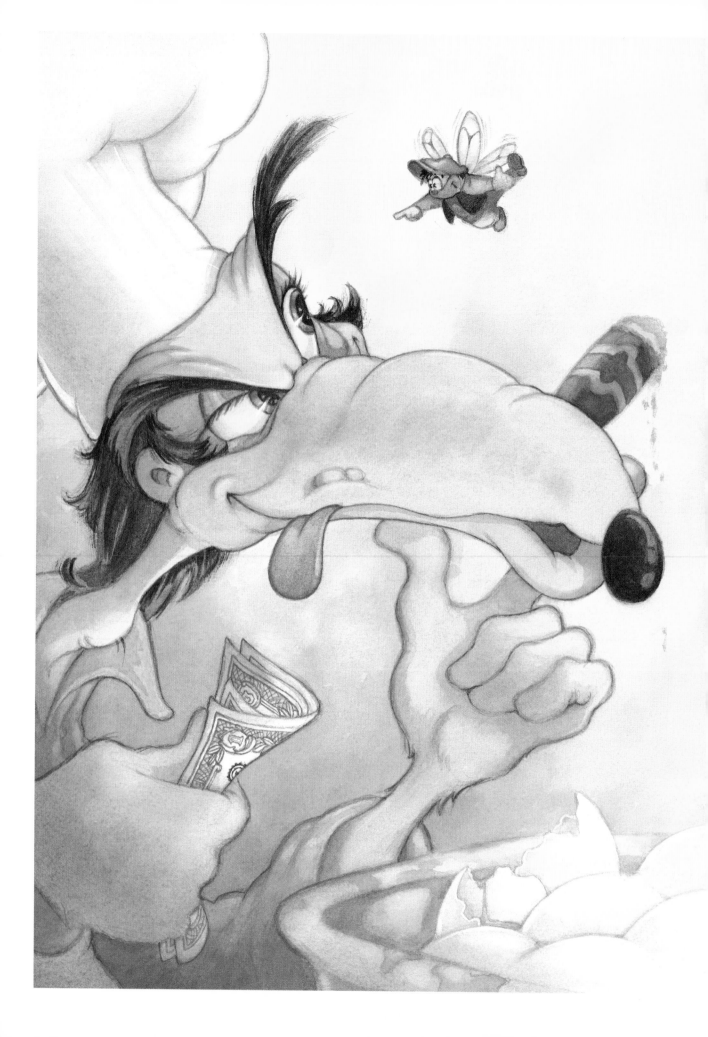

We'll create a diversion,
draw them out to the street
singing "Ice cream, free ice cream,
free ice cream to eat.

And while they're outside,
before they get back,
Boss, you'll perform
your hijack attack."

"Nice work!" beams Rat
"Now let's away,
to distract three young men
from their work with our play."

So slowly and slyly
to Dicky's they near,
singing "Ice cream! Free ice cream!"
for the kids to hear.

"Free ice cream!" squeal the Buddies.
"That offer can't be beat!"
They forget their "noble trust"
and all run to the street.

While they look all around
for the ice cream man,
the egg snatching weasel
completes his foul plan.

He reaches in the nest
with his greedy green arm
lifting Dicky's sleeping brother
from the nest where he's warm.

He tells this unborn egg,
as he's told so many ducks,
"I truly hate to do this
but I really love the bucks!"

Outside Dicky puzzles,
"No ice-cream man would hide."
With an ambiance of nonchalance,
he saunters back inside.

But Bo Bo wants that ice cream
so he climbs the light post.
Way up high where a guy
can always see the most.

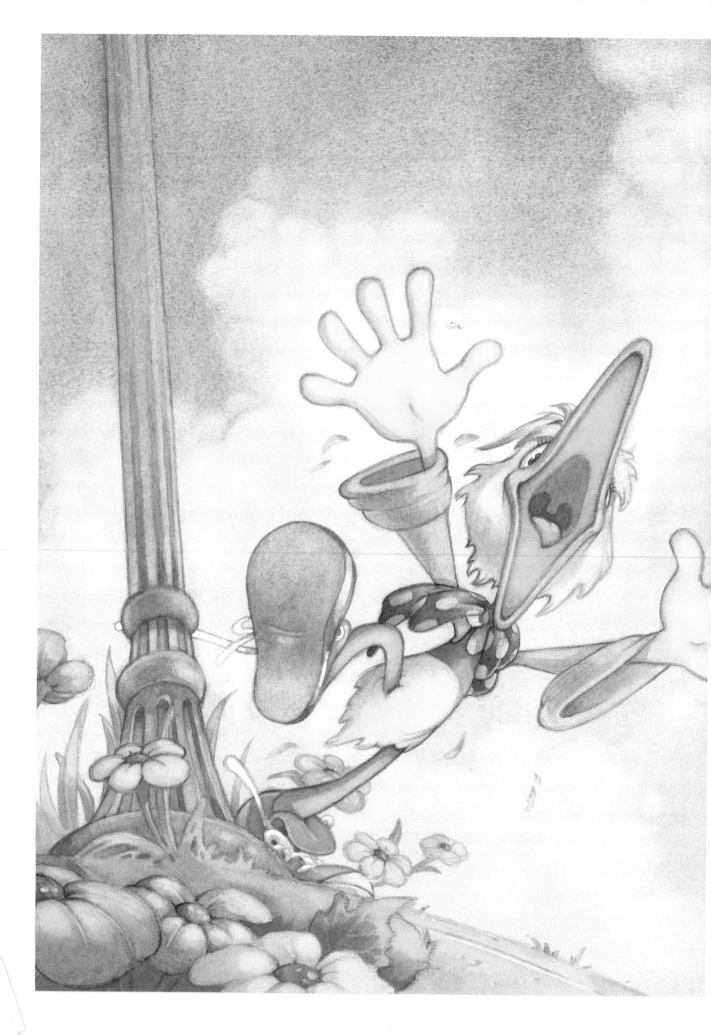

Back out the front door
flailing and flapping,
streaks Dicky Duck,
megaphonic beak quacking.

"We left him alone
and now the egg's gone!"
He cries, "Where has he gone?
He can't be gone long!"

Atop his watchtower
Bo Bo's keen eyes search.
Down the hill a lone figure
lurks in the lurch.

"Hey! That guy's got our egg!
And the problem's not minor!
He just took your brother
in the Atomic Egg Diner!!!"

"The Atomic Egg Diner!"
Dicky cries "What'll we do?"
At this moment it would seem
Dicky's brother is through.

Then Bo Bo squares his shoulders,
and he stands erect,
and his friends understand,
they're here to protect.

They run to Dicky's skateboard.
They quickly mount their steed.
They fire up the rockets to
the top end, red line speed.

A mighty surge is felt
from the power jets below
that blasts the Buddies down the hill
"To the rescue here we go!"

As the Rat lifts the egg
for the fatal crack . . .
Crash! Through the kitchen
comes the piggyback attack.

Cages, hens, and eggs
fly everywhere
and Dicky's little brother
goes straight in the air.

"My brother!" cries Dicky,
"Don't let him fall!
All for one!
And one for all!"

Are these knights too late?
The egg has left the hand!
Dicky dives — and saves his brother
an inch before he's panned.

Bo Bo wields a mighty sword
of tempered stale French bread,
bashing at the bulbous beeze
of greedy Weeze's head!

Jack liberates the hens
in an act of chivalry.
Rat's knocked out with his hot frying pan
and away the Buddies flee.

Relieved, having rescued the baby,
triumphant from their crusade,
with the egg in hand of the brave little band,
straight for their home they made.

They take it back to the nursery,
tuck it safely in its nest.
And it lies there very quietly —
the thing an egg does best.

Just then from deep inside
comes a gentle mumble rumble.
Two webbed feet pop out,
and the shell starts to crumble.

Pop! The egg opens.
What a surprise!
This duckling is pretty
with big blue eyes.

And make no mistake,
that's the way it goes.

Dicky didn't get a brother
but a new sister, Rose.

And the Buddies three, quite gallantly,
protected Rose's rights.
As in days of old, when knights were bold,
today was a day for knights.